WEiRDo

Scholastic Children's Books
An imprint of Scholastic Ltd
Euston House, 24 Eversholt Street, London, NW1 1DB, UK
Registered office: Westfield Road, Southam, Warwickshire, CV47 0RA
SCHOLASTIC and associated logos are trademarks and/or
registered trademarks of Scholastic Inc.

Weirdo first published by Scholastic Australia, 2013
Text copyright © Anh Do, 2013
Illustrations copyright © Jules Faber, 2013

Weirdo 2: Even Weirder first published by Scholastic Australia, 2014
Text copyright © Anh Do, 2014
Illustrations copyright © Jules Faber, 2014

This collection first published in the UK by Scholastic Ltd, 2019

The right of Anh Do and Jules Faber to be identified as the
author and illustrator of this work has been asserted.

ISBN 978 1407 19955 9

A CIP catalogue record for this book
is available from the British Library.

Printed by CPI Group (UK) Ltd, Croydon CR0 4YY
Papers used by Scholastic Children's Books are made
from wood grown in sustainable forests.

1 3 5 7 9 10 8 6 4 2

BLAH.
BLAH.
BLAH

www.scholastic.co.uk

ANH DO

Illustrated by JULES FABER

WEiRDO

SCHOLASTIC

CHAPTER 1

Here we go again. Even in a **new school**, in a **new town**, my year is about to start the **exact** same way it always does . . .

WHAT'S YOUR NAME?

WEIR.

"That's an interesting name. What's your last name?" says Miss Franklin.

That's the bit I **really** hate. Why does **everyone** have to ask for your **last name**?

"Weir, what's your last name?" she asks again.

DO.

DO?
RHYMES WITH "GO"?

UH-HUH . . .

"Your name's . . . Weir *Do*? It's not really, is it?"

"Yes, actually, it is," I reply.

WEIRDO?

Get ready for it. In exactly **three** seconds, all the kids will start laughing . . .

ONE,
TWO,
THR—

HAHAHAHA!

That's the story of my life!

SO WHAT'S YOUR SISTER'S
NAME? PLAY?

→ PLAY DO!

HA HA HA

WHAT'S YOUR FATHER'S
NAME? TAE KWON?

↘ TAE KWON DO!

HA HA HA

What I would give for a last name like **Smith** or **Jones** or **Chapman** or **Fletcher**. Anything! Even **GoopGoop** goes better with Weir than Do.

What's your name?

Weir GOOPGOOP!

YAY!

I guess when they gave out last names,

I lost . . . big time.

Thing is, my dad was born in Vietnam. His last name is **Do**. (Yep, rhymes with "go".)

My mum's last name before she married my dad was **Weir**. She really loved that name, so I got lumped with Weir Do! **WEIRDO!**

LuCKy Me!

My parents could have given me any first name at all, like **John, Kevin, Shmevin,**

ANYTHING!

What about Rusty? **Rusty Do** sounds like a movie star.

I'd like to thank my parents for my cool name!

Or maybe a famous country music singer.

I'm glad I'm not a Weirdoooooooooooo

Instead, I'm stuck with the **worst** name since **Mrs Face** called her son **Butt**.

Now that was a **funny** roll call:

☑ Kevin Clark
☑ Mary Connors
☐ Butt Face

HA HA HA HA

Anyway, back to class . . .

"Children, it's **rude** to laugh at someone's name," says the teacher. "I'm sorry, Weir . . . Do. Please sit down, Weir . . . DO."

And then it started.

I could tell the teacher was trying **really hard** not to laugh. It's a sign when people's cheeks puff up like they're about to **explode**.

I'm actually an expert on the subject.

I've seen it **a lot**.

My kindergarten teacher

My first-grade teacher

My second-grade teacher

The day I was born . . .

WHAT'S HIS NAME?

Finally, my new teacher ran out of the classroom . . .

BWA HA HAHA, HAHAHA HA HAHA!

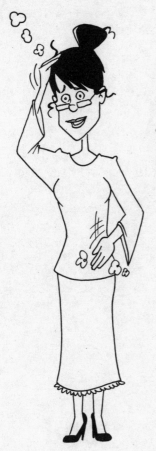

then she returned.

PLEASE TAKE A SEAT, WEIR . . .

I was so busy trying not to look embarrassed, I forgot I was wearing my sister's old shoes . . .

and

tripped._

That's when a **girl** reached down

to help me up.

As I looked into her face, I thought she was the

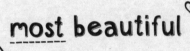 **most beautiful** ♡❤

girl in the world.

Her pencil case read

Bella Allen.

CHAPTER 2

I guess I should tell you a bit about my family.

My sister's name is Sally.

Why did *she* get the normal name? Not that **I'd** like to be called **Sally**.

Sally Do

Me

Sally is older than me by three years and she is one of those people who always saves up her Easter eggs for months and months. It used to be great finding her **hidden** pile of eggs in **June!**

But last year, she'd had enough of me eating her stash, so she invented a way to make sure I **never** touched them again.

Sally also likes to bug me with some
really annoying habits.

DON'T COPY ME. → DON'T COPY ME.

GO AWAY. → GO AWAY.

ARGHHHH! → ARGHHHH!

Then Dad gave me some tips on how to get her back.

SALLY IS SMELLY.

SALLY IS SMELL—

HAHA HAHAHA!

But then she figured out a way around it.

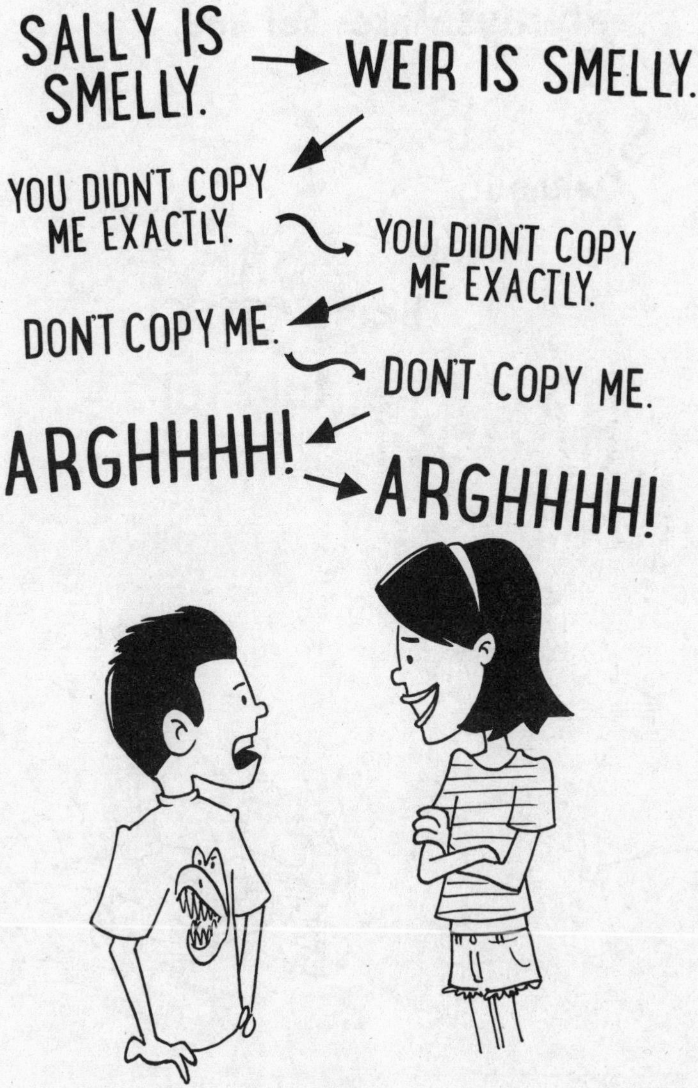

Sally's also one of those people who

<u>**always**</u> makes her bed . . .

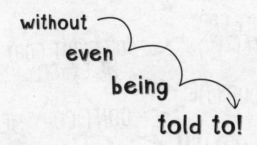

without
even
being
told to!

Sally's bed

My bed

In fact, almost **everything** she does makes me look **bad.**

Sally's wardrobe

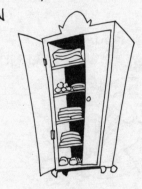

My wardrobe

Sally's homework

My homework

My little brother's name is **Roger**.

Another normal name, but read on ⟫⟫⟫

he's **NOT** normal.

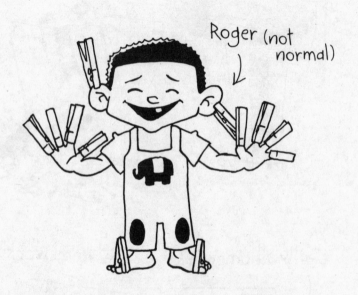

Roger (not normal)

He has just become tall enough to use the toilet instead of his potty. But it's not going so well so far. For the **third time** this week, he's slammed the toilet seat on his **thing** . . .

He's also been dipping stuff in his baby food.
Often **stuff that is important.**

PHONE WANT
EAT PUDDING?

Roger is just starting to talk, and some words come out **funny**. Like when he tries to say **Father**, it sounds more like something else.

SAY
"FATHER."

BIG FARTER!
BIG FARTER!

Big Farter is actually a good way to describe Dad.

My dad is one of those dads who tells you not to **pass gas** in public, but then when he feels like it, he just goes ahead and **FARTS**.

RRRRRIIPPP!!!

If Mum's nearby, Dad will try to blame it on something else that **couldn't possibly** have made such a **big** noise.

Like...

IT WAS
THE BIRD

HUH?

Or . . .

But if Mum's not around and it's just us kids,
Dad likes to **boast**.

FEEL THAT EARTHQUAKE, KIDS?

And here's a tip, if my dad ever asks you to pull his finger . . .

DON'T!

Just run the other way!

PULL MY FINGER . . .

If you're **too slow**, it's time to get out the **clothespins**.

Here's my mum. She's one of those people who **loves** to save money. I don't want to call her **cheap** . . . but she is.

She won't even let me change the water after Roger has a bath. And if Roger's been playing in the **dirt** all day, I think I come out **dirtier** than when I went in.

But **the worst** thing she does is she **licks** her hand to **fix up my hair**.

WEIR, COME HERE, YOU'VE GOT A HAIR OUT OF PLACE.

'SLURP!

Great. Now I look like the **world's biggest nerd** and **smell** like the **tuna sandwich** Mum had at lunch.

Mum's cheapness also explains why I was wearing **my sister's shoes** on the first day of school.

They don't really fit yet, but Mum says they will encourage my feet to grow.

As if shoes speak to feet!

CMON. FEETY FEETY. YOU NEED TO GROW NOW.

NUH.

The **craziest** person in our family is **Granddad**.
He is Mum's dad and he is

really, really, really old.

He is so old, sometimes bits of him just

fall
out.

WHAT'S THIS IN
MY SOUP?

OH. THAT'S WHERE MY
ROBOTIC EAR WENT!

But he always pops
everything back in place.

SQUELCH!

If I got to choose robotic parts, I'd get some **really fast legs**. I'm not a very fast runner. When they handed out **fast running**, I lost out.

I lost out on **tallness**, too.

And on **good hair**.

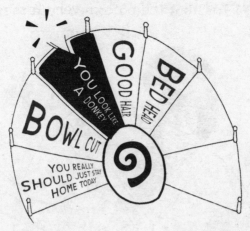

I'm a bit different, I won't lie. **WEIRDO's**
not just my name. It kind of **describes the
way I am** . . .

Like, whenever I eat a hamburger, the meat **always** falls out the bottom. I hate that.

And whenever I pull off a plaster, I always **rip off my scab**, too.

I can't eat the **stringy** stuff on the inside of a banana. That stuff tastes **strange**.

But **I LIKE** lots of weird things, too, like when it's **hot** at night and you turn your pillow over, the other side is **nice and COOL!**

Like an **extra** pillow! **I love that!**

I also like it when you have to **PEE REALLY BADLY** and you find a toilet just in time.

AAAAAHH!

Or when there's an ad break on your **favourite** TV show, and you run out to do something really important, but then you come back **just in time!**

It's also great when you mix up a packet of **cheesy macaroni**, and halfway through eating it, you get that one

→ bright orange macaroni bit

with

stacks of flavour

stuck on it!

YAY!

But most of all, **I love to draw!**

I like drawing

anything,

anywhere.

I even like drawing on the steamy mirror after a bath.

What I like drawing the most are animals. **Not just any animals**, but

WEIRD animals.

I like to mix them up!

My favourite is a **duck** crossed with a **poodle**:

Duck + Poodle = DOODLE!

Or a **fish** crossed with a **cat**:

Fish + Cat
= FAT!

Or a **frog** crossed with a **pug**:

Frog + Pug
= FRUG!

At the end of the day, things aren't too bad.
There are some things that I'm **GOOD AT**.

Like **spelling** . . .

And **remembering people's names**.

I do this by making a | **picture** | in my mind of something that **rhymes** with a person's name.

Like I remembered the name of a girl from my old school called **Alana Stead** by thinking of the words **Banana Head**.

Butt Face

Of course **Mrs Face's** kid is **easy!**

CHAPTER 3

Let's get back to my first day in my new school.

The bell rang for outdoor lunch, and I followed everyone out into the playground.

I could see it was a normal playground with all the normal silliness.

HOW TO:
Smell the cheese

BOOYAH!

I can't believe some kids still fall for that!

HOW TO: Arm Burn

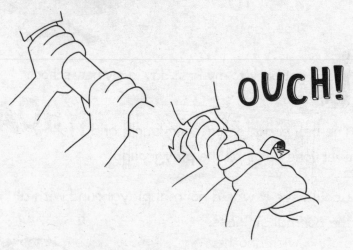

HOW TO: Wedgie

HOW TO:
Shoe Lacing

WHOA!

I looked over to the corner and saw *Bella Allen* sitting with another girl from our class. It looked like she was about to get a **Wet Finger** in her ear!

I rushed over to save her but **tripped** and **fell** again!

Stupid shoes!

So I called out from the ground . . .

BELLA! WATCH OUT!

She turned and—

WET
FINGER!

Oh **NO!** I just caused Bella to get a **poke** in the eye.

I ran away and hid. ~

That afternoon we had our first gym lesson with **Mr McDool**. His name is **easy** to remember.

Mr McDool told us we were going to have our very own **class Olympics**. To make it seem more real, he even lit an old candle and called it the **Olympic torch**. He held it up high and some wax tipped out,

burning his armpit.

OUCH!

Mr McDool made ribbons to give out for first, second and third in the running races. I wish they had ribbons for **second last**.

I'm **really good**
at coming in **second last**.

I've learned to hang back in the running course.
Don't line up along a bunch of guys who look fast.
Line up near the end with the guys who look
slow.

You can tell │**slow guys**│ by a few surefire signs.

Socks   Trousers   Finger   Finger
pulled   pulled   always   always in
up too   up too   in nose.   someone
high.   high.   else's nose.

But usually the best way to tell who's the slowest is by finding the guy who's got the top bit of his **butt crack** showing. He's almost **always** going to be slow.

In my new class, that kid's name was **Toby Hogan**. The others were calling him **Piggy Bank** because it looked like his **butt crack** was a **coin slot**. He was the **perfect** choice to race with.

Well, someone must have put a

– **hundred** dollars

in the coin slot before Toby's run, because it
turned out

Toby Hogan was

super fast! >>>>

← Me! Second last again!

We were standing around waiting for a row of girls to race when a kid called Josh Keenan started showing off his arm muscles. Before I knew what was happening, it turned into a **muscle contest**.

Great, another contest for me to come  in.

Or worse, last!

I tried to walk away, but it was too late. It would've looked like I was **chickening out**. Everyone's muscles were going to be bigger than mine.

So when it was my turn, I did the

very best flex I could manage.

Toby Hogan

64

WHOOO!

They didn't know I was doing
a trick that Dad showed me . . .

It was going so well that I started **showing off** and turning so that all the **girls** could see.

That's when Toby Hogan saw what I was doing and **busted** me.

Then they all started **shouting**:

LIAR, LIAR, PANTS ON FIRE!

I thought they were just saying it 'cause it rhymes, but it turns out they weren't. I'd backed into **Mr McDool's Olympic torch** and **my pants really were** on fire!

Mr McDool chucked a bucket of water on me to put it out.

There's that look again . . . he's trying not to laugh!

I stood there **dripping wet** while my whole class, including *Bella Allen*, stared at me like I was a complete . . .

weirdo.

The fire **burned a hole** right in the middle of my school shorts. For the rest of the day, I had to walk around sideways with my back to the wall so no one could see my *frog* undies.

I couldn't wait till the bell at the end of the first day. When Mum came to pick me up, I ran to her as fast as I could.

When I ran past Bella, she called out, **"Nice frogs!"**

UGH!

I went blank! Half my brain wanted to call back: **"Frogs are the best."** The other half wanted to say: **"Frogs are the coolest."** But it came out all wrong.

FROGS ARE THE BOOLEST!

ARGHHHHHH!

Boolest! Who says **Boolest???!!!**

What a way to start the new year!

CHAPTER 4

The next day at school, there was **awesome news.** Another new kid was starting. Since I had been there a **whole day already**, he was now the **new guy**.

And when he walked in, it got **even better**.

the ^new new guy!

I thought to myself, **YES!**

This guy makes me look

SUPER <u>normal!</u>

He's going to take some of the attention off me . . .

and I was right!

Henry quickly became the **strangest** guy in the class. He did everything a bit **differently**. Like when you said his name, it took three tries before he'd turn around.

HENRY!
HENRY!!
HENRY!!!

HUH?

And he has his own versions of nursery rhymes . . .

Mary had a little lamb,
who one day just
dropped dead.
Now it goes to school
with her,
Between two chunks
of bread.

Well, the other kids think he's **strange**, but I think he's pretty **funny**.

That afternoon, I found myself standing in line outside the HEAD TEACHER's office. Henry was there, too.

HI. HENRY.

HENRY!

HENRY!

HI. WEIR!

HEAD TEACHER

Turns out we were both there because of one guy ⟶ **Blake Green**. It hadn't taken us long to figure out that just about everything that Blake Green tells you to do, **you shouldn't do**.

When Blake first saw Henry, he got the same look on his face that a dog gets when it looks at your ham sandwich.

dog

ham sandwich

Henry

Blake Green

Henry told me what Blake Green made him do. Henry was there because Blake tricked him into going into the **girls' bathroom**.

HEY, WHERE DID MY SCHOOLBAG GO?

IT'S OVER THERE. GO HAVE A LOOK.

THANKS!

Here's what happened to **me**:

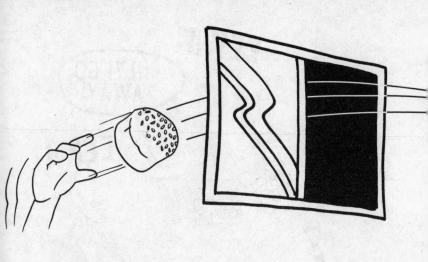

I managed to get **three** teachers angry with **one** bread roll.

When it was my turn to go into the head teacher's office, Henry did something I **wasn't** expecting.

MR HARRIS. WEIR DIDN'T MEAN TO THROW THE BREAD ROLL THROUGH THE WINDOW. HE TRIPPED IN HIS SISTER'S SHOES AND HIS LUNCH WENT FLYING OUT OF HIS HANDS.

He helped me out!

So I thought I ought to help him out, too.

HENRY WAS JUST LOOKING FOR HIS SCHOOLBAG. BLAKE TOLD HIM IT WAS IN THE BATHROOM. HE DIDN'T REALIZE IT WAS THE GIRLS' BATHROOM. HE'S NEW.

We **grinned** at each other, both convinced that we were

<u>out</u>

of trouble.

We were <u>wrong.</u>

But when we walked in, I got the
best surprise of my life!

Bella was in detention, too! She was in
trouble for accidentally elbowing the girl who
stuck a **finger** in her **ear!**

Bella is easily the **prettiest** girl in the class.
Well, whenever Jenny, Clare, Mary, Sue, Yana
and Wendy are away.

Bella!

Jenny Clare Mary Sue Yana Wendy

But I liked her. I liked her **a lot!**

And it turned out Henry liked her, too!

As soon as we walked in, he tried out one of his **super smooth**, **talking-to-girls** tricks:

HI. BELLA.
WANT TO HEAR
MY SPECIAL
NURSERY RHYME?

There was a little bunny, Whose nose was very runny. If you think it's very funny, well, it's SNOT!

Bella moved away from Henry and closer to me. That's when I realized that with Henry as my sidekick, **I'd always be the cool one!**

cool one

So that's how me and Henry became

best friends.

For the rest of the week, me and Henry got up to <u>loads</u> of **funny business.**

I CAN MAKE YOU FALL OVER WITH THE POWER OF MY MIND.

Henry thinks my drawings are **cool**, so I've been making some **really funny** ones for him:

Frilled-neck lizard

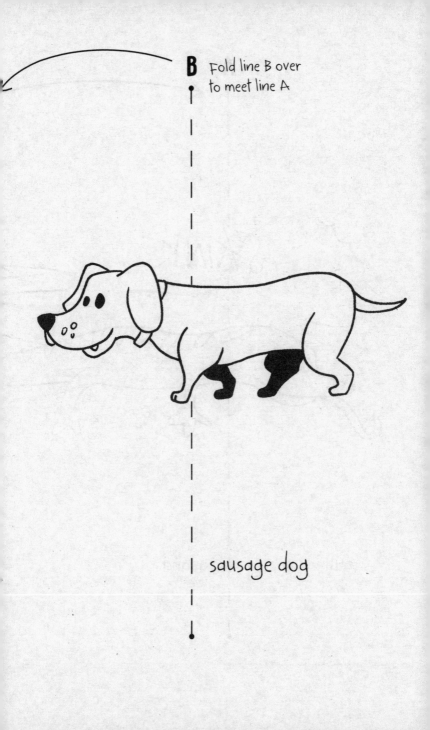

B Fold line B over to meet line A

sausage dog

A

SKINK

B Same again!

skunk

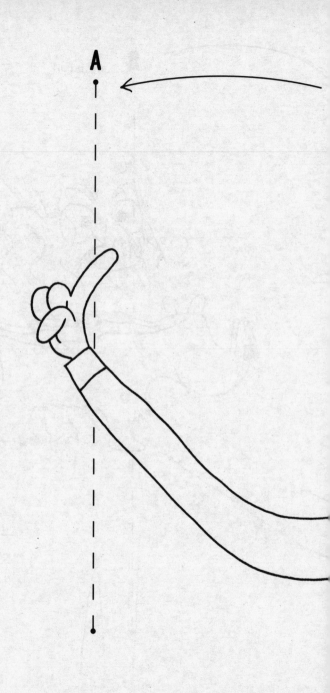

A

CHAPTER 6

The head teacher, Mr Harris, came in to talk to our class about a **very important** matter.

"Kids, we've recently discovered that many of you have animals living in your hair called **lice**."

Animals living in my hair?! At first, I thought:

HOW COOL!

But it turns out, these things are not so good for you. They're tiny insects that **suck your blood** and make your head **itchy**.

RARR!

Mr Harris then told us all to line up so some **lice inspectors** could check our heads.

I really hoped these guys didn't **check for worms** as well, because I wanted to keep my trousers on.

They told us that if your head was **itchy**, it meant you probably had **lice**.

As soon as they said this, my head felt itchy, but I didn't want to scratch it. I think everyone felt the same. We all stood there with **itchy** heads that we were

too afraid to scratch!

At the end of it, Mr Harris told us that **we all had lice.**

The **whole** class!

We were each given a bottle of shampoo and told to stay home **(yay!)** until we'd really washed our hair.

Then he told us that these **creatures** were brought to school by someone carrying them in their hair, and it all started a few days ago.

Well, **of course** everyone right away turned to Henry. He'd just turned up a few days ago, and he had this **guilty** look on his face.

guilty

It **must've** been him!

I'd just made a new friend, and now he was the **lice guy!** I'd have to stay away from him . . .

It felt like this one time Mum let me choose a Transformer for Christmas, then she wrapped it up and I couldn't have it for a month!

Suddenly, we heard some **chirping** noises in the classroom.

meep meep

At first, I thought it was my **sister** hiding in the locker with the **hiccups**.

No one knew what the noise was. So Miss Franklin told us all to go around the classroom and look for the **mysterious** noise.

We looked for ages, but **found nothing.**

Then Henry put up his hand.

MISS, IT SOUNDS LIKE BABY SPARROWS.

"How do you know that, Henry?"
said Miss Franklin.

"We had **lots** of birds on our farm, so I know what they sound like."

"Do you know where they are?" the teacher asked.

"Sparrows like to nest up high," said Henry.
"I think they're **in the ceiling**."

Next, the school called some **bird inspectors** to come to our classroom and check the ceiling. And, sure enough, **Henry was right.**

There was a nest up there, and not only that, it was the sparrows who were responsible for everyone's lice.

They found **lots** of **bird lice** in the nest!

Henry became the

class hero for solving

The Mystery of the Chirping Noise

and everyone also realized that it wasn't
him who gave us all lice.

All of a sudden I was **best friends** with the

coolest kid
in the class.

DON'T FORGET
I WAS HIS
FRIEND FIRST!

The very next day, Henry was back to being himself.

LOOK AT ME. I'M A WALRUS.

Oh well, at least I have him **all to myself again.**

It was **show-and-tell** day, and I decided to take my **robotic ninja hamster** to school. He looked pretty dirty and needed a wash, so I turned on the sink tap and heard a **huge** <u>**scream!**</u>

Sally

EEEEEEEKK!

WHO TURNED ON THE TAP????

Sally was in the middle of a shower. **Oops.**
So when she came out, she got me back by
tying my school trousers together.
When I went to put them on, I fell and
<u>banged</u> my head!

So I got her back by
putting glue in her shoes.

At school, Bella spent all of lunch handing out invitations to her **birthday party**.

Everyone in my class got an invitation.

Everyone except me.

When she was handing them out and she got to me, she smiled and then walked right past.

She even gave one to Toby Hogan. She must have liked what he brought in for show-and-tell.

THIS IS WHAT YOU CALL A PIGGY BANK.

Even **Henry** got an invitation!

Henry's toilet paper-dispensing helmet

WOOHOO!

What a bummer. She must have thought my **robotic ninja hamster** was weird. **Just like me**. Could this day get any **worse?**

After school, I heard Mum on the phone talking to Bella's mum! Then Mum gave me the **worst news I could _ever_ hear**.

BELLA'S MUM HAS TO TAKE HER GRANDMA TO THE DOCTOR THIS AFTERNOON, SO BELLA IS COMING OVER TO OUR HOUSE. ISN'T THAT NICE?

NOOOOOOOO!!!!!!

No one's been over to my house yet. Not even Henry. **My family is <u>too</u> weird!** But it was too late, and before I knew it,

Bella was at our front door.

"This is Weir's granddad, Bob," said my mum.

HELLO THERE, HOW ABOUT A HUG FOR AN OLD MAN?

OH NO, I've seen him do this before!

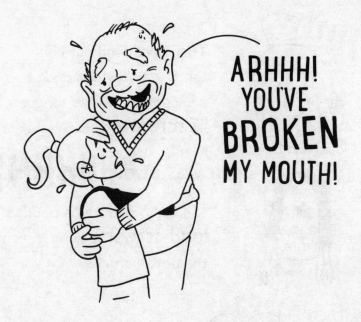

ARHHH! YOU'VE BROKEN MY MOUTH!

"Sorry about that, Bella!" said my mum.

"Just kidding!" said Granddad. "They come out. Look. Isn't that cool?"

Then Granddad put his teeth in backward and accidentally bit his tongue. He **screamed**.

AHHHHH!

Suddenly, there was another **loud scream**, coming from the bathroom.

OWWW!

UH-OH, IT SOUNDS LIKE ROGER'S SLAMMED THE TOILET SEAT ON HIS **THING** AGAIN.

WHAT DOES SHE
MEAN BY HIS
"THING"?

I don't like making stuff up, but in this
case, **I had to.**

HE LIKES TO CALL HIS HAND A "THING." LIKE RAHHHH, HAND THINGY.

My family is like one **disaster** waiting to happen after another!

Then my **worst fear** happened. Dad came home early from work. He walked right up to me and said the **baddest** thing he could say.

PULL MY FINGER!

DAD, NOOOOOO!!!

But it turns out he wasn't going to **embarrass** me after all.

PLEASE, I'VE GOT A CRAMP IN MY HAND!

So Mum gave Dad a quick hand massage.

Too many **close calls** so far, but overall, things were still all right.

Me and Bella were talking about the toys we'd brought in for show-and-tell. My **ninja hamster** was giving her **scientist doll** a ride on his back.

That's when Sally came out of her room.

Oh no, I forgot about the glue I put in her shoes!

She marched right up to where me and Bella were sitting.

NOOOOOOO!

My life is
destroyed!

But then Bella said something that I didn't expect at all!

HEY, THAT'S KINDA COOL. MY SCHOOLBAG USED TO BELONG TO MY BROTHER.

HUH?

WOW. This is **actually** going **great!**

I was just starting to feel really good about things when the doorbell rang . . . **What now?!**

I looked down the
hallway and saw **Henry**
at the door!

WHAT ARE
YOU DOING,
HENRY?

I'M WAITING FOR
YOU TO LET ME IN!

"But why are you wearing
THAT?!" I asked him.

"Because I have a co—"

AH-CHOO

OOO!

Henry's **big green booger** hit me in the eye!

I turned and accidentally **knocked Bella over.** That's when the **booger** flew from my face onto Bella's!

YUCK!

I tried to wipe it off her with Henry's toilet paper.

And that's when I spotted **Roger running down the hall**

with

Bella's

doll!

I **panicked** and couldn't think properly. I turned to Bella and probably said the **uncoolest** thing you could say to a girl.

UH, ME NEED GO PEE-PEE NOW!

I raced after Roger, but by the time I got to his room, it was **too late**.

DOLL EAT PUDDING.

The doll's head was covered in **yellow goop!**

What do I do <u>now</u>?!?!

Sally and Henry raced in after me.

QUICK, GET SOME WATER TO WASH HER.

I ran back out to the kitchen, where Bella was sitting and filled up two cups of water. She looked at me **confused**.

UH, I LIKE TO DRINK TWO CUPS OF WATER BEFORE I GO TO THE TOILET . . .

IT HELPS ME GO PEE-PEE.

OKAAAAAY.

When I got back to Roger's room, there was pudding **everywhere!**

QUICK,
TO THE BATHROOM!

I grabbed the doll and ran to the bathroom. Sally and Henry followed.

Granddad was in there and we **squeezed** past him to get to the sink.

We were all hovering over the doll when Mum, Bella's mum, and Bella walked in to see what all the **fuss** was about.

Granddad tried to explain . . .

WE FOUND A COUPLE
OF **LICE** ON BELLA'S DOLL.
SO WE'VE JUST GIVEN HER A
LITTLE HAIR WASH WITH
THIS **LICE SHAMPOO**.

We cleaned up the doll just in time to hand her
back to Bella.

OH. THANK YOU FOR DOING THAT.

It was time to say bye to Bella, and I was sure she thought I was **even weirder** than before, thanks to my **crazy** family.

BYE, WEIR. YOUR FAMILY IS **REALLY** FUNNY!

Then she pulled an envelope out of
her schoolbag.

I DIDN'T WANT TO GIVE
THIS TO YOU IN
FRONT OF EVERYONE
AT SCHOOL.

It was an **invitation** to her birthday party
that she'd drawn herself.

I LOVE **FROGS**, TOO. I THINK THEY'RE THE **BOOLEST!**

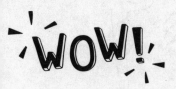

A **special birthday invitation** from the **seventh-best-looking girl** at school.

This could be . . .

the **B.E.S.T** year ever!

MORE
TO COME!

For my three **favourite**

WeirDos!

FROM ANH

Xavier, Luc, and Leon

DEDICATIONS

WEiRDO²

EVEN WEIRDER!

ANH DO

Illustrated by JULES FABER

WEiRDO²

EVEN WEIRDER!

CHAPTER 1

I was out shopping for a **birthday present** for the seventh-best-looking girl in the class. So why did I have five years' worth of **toilet paper** in the trolley?

Because
my life is
<u>weird.</u>

If something's on sale at the store, Mum will buy **lots** of it.

And guess what was on sale today?

That's right,

toilet paper.

There we all were . . . looking like

the family that has the

in the world.

The fact is, we don't just use toilet paper in the bathroom. We use it for other **stuff** around the house . . .

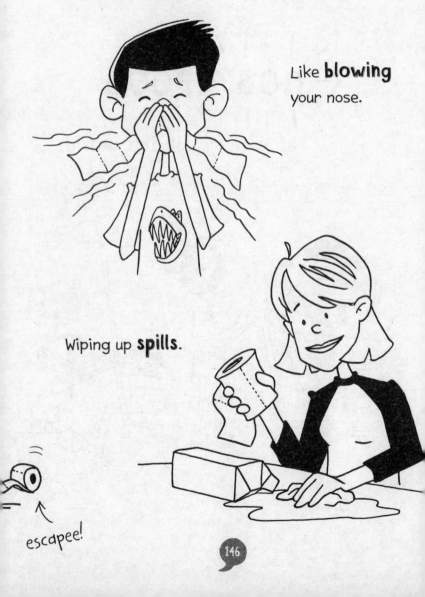

Like **blowing** your nose.

Wiping up **spills**.

escapee!

Ten pin bowling.

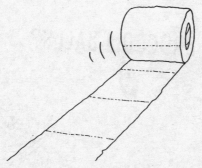

Did I tell you my mum was **thrifty**? She's one of those people who gets a little too excited about the lady in the corner of the shop giving out the **free sausage samples**.

SMILE!

Mum will make us **all line up** for a taste, no matter what the sample is.

BROCCOLI BALLS?

YUMMO!

DUCK DOUGHNUT?

WOW WEE!

You're only allowed **one** sausage per person, but Mum makes us walk away and then come back looking slightly different, just to get **more food**.

And if the sausages are **REALLY** tasty, she'll make us come back one **extra time**.

GREAT!
NOW WE DON'T HAVE TO WORRY ABOUT LUNCH!

Roger's **the worst** at shopping. Somehow **strange stuff** always ends up in the trolley when he's around.

WHO BOUGHT THESE CRISPS AND JUMBO SAFETY PINS?

151

guilty

WHO BOUGHT THIS ITCHY BUTT CREAM?

guilty

Anyway, there we were at the checkout with our

2,000

rolls of toilet paper, when I looked across
and saw ... **BELLA ALLEN!**

HI, WEIR!

HI, BELLA.

"What are you buying?" she asked.

"We're just buying a . . . birthday present for you," I replied.

"Is that my present behind your back?" she asked with a smile.

"Oh, no, that isn't for you either."

I brought out the **itchy butt cream** to show her.

SEE? THIS IS JUST, UMM, JUST IN CASE . . . CHEAP TOILET PAPER CAN BE A BIT ROUGH SOMETIMES!

ITCHY BUTT CREAM

What was I saying?!

"Okaaaaay, bye, Weir," she said.

NOOOOO!

Now Bella Allen thinks I am **the king of poop**. That I need a trolley full of toilet paper all for myself!

Can my life get any **worse?**

PRICE CHECK ON
EXTRA-LARGE
ITCHY BUTT CREAM
FOR THE WEIRDO
AT CHECKOUT FIVE.

My life **just got worse!**

Now the **whole** supermarket's looking at me!

How did the lady at the checkout know my name? Must have been

 a lucky guess!

CHAPTER 2

My first name is **Weir**. My last name is **Do**. (Yep, rhymes with "go".)

Just in case you missed my first book, let me tell you a little bit about me and my family.

Dad

Mum (thrifty)

Granddad

Me

Roger

Sally

toilet paper

You already know I'm a **bit weird**. Like when they handed out **talents**, I wound up with . . .

And when they handed out **family hobbies** . . .

And you already know that my mum is thrifty.
She **really** is.

For **Roger's birthday**, instead of paying for
real helium balloons that float up to the
ceiling . . .

. . . she just blew up plain balloons and then **stuck** them to the ceiling with **sticky tape**.

She's also one of those mums who makes us wear **hand-me-down** clothes. I got stuck with Sally's **old school shoes** . . . but at least I didn't get her sweater!

My sister, Sally, is **super** neat. She does

<u>everything</u>
perfectly.

She even peels an orange all in **one go**.

perfect

And she's really good at making things,
like **balloon** animals.

orange peel

Sally **never** makes
a mess eating her
noodles.

But me, I always seem to get that one long noodle that goes on and on for ever!

At least I'm not as **messy** as Roger. Sometimes he even ends up with noodles

coming out of his nose.

Roger is my little brother, and he likes to **destroy stuff**. This week he's been **throwing** things into the bath. To **"clean"** them.

Often important things . .

Mum refused to waste the soggy bread . . . and I have to say, the **soggy sandwich** was one of the **worst three sandwiches** I've ever had in my life.

soggy sandwich

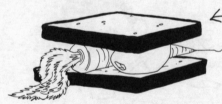

← 2nd worst sandwich
(carrot and tomato)

number 1 worst
sandwich ever
(pig ears)

My dad is **just plain strange**.

He can do a **burp** that lasts for a looooo...ng time!

169

UURRR

still going!

171

RRRRRP

finally finished!

Dad can also **fart** from the **front door** to the **back door**, but we won't go into that.

The other thing Dad likes to do is **dance really badly**. He tries to copy people on TV.

horsey dance

worm dance

robot dance

still the
worm dance

Finally, there's Granddad. His teeth come out, and his body parts make **funny** noises . . .

WHOOP WHOOP!

And he likes to play **silly** tricks.

《SHAKE》 HANDS?

ZZZZZ
ZZZZZ
ZZZZZZ!

HAHA
HAHA HA

He also pulls his trousers up **really high**, which is the opposite of some of the **cool** kids at school.

Granddad—high

Joey Keenan—low

Toby Hogan—super lo

Even our **pet bird** is weird. Most birds like to make happy chirpy noises. But **Blockhead** always makes strange sounds, like . . .

WOOF WOOF!

And sometimes . . .

MOOO!

And if he's eaten some **funny birdseed**, he'll say . . .

WANNA FIGHT?

Henry's my best friend from school. He doesn't care that I'm weird, or that I like to draw silly pictures.

Like this one . . .

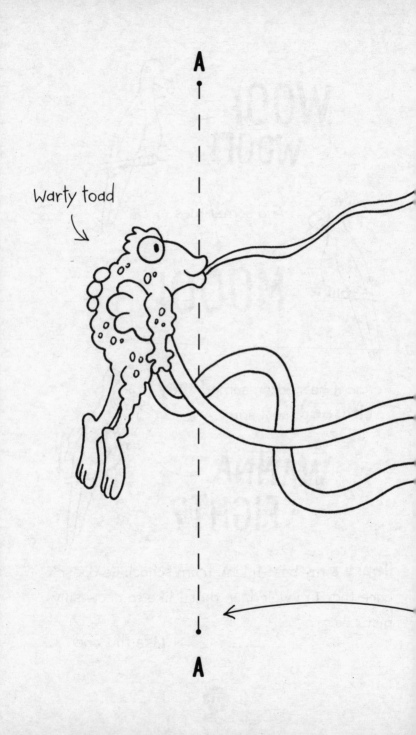

Warty toad

B

Blake

Fold line B over
to meet line A

B

Me and Henry like to make up new words for things, too . . . like **"Finkles."**

That's the word we invented for the **wrinkles** you get on your **fingers** when you've sat in the bath

for

<u>too</u>

long.

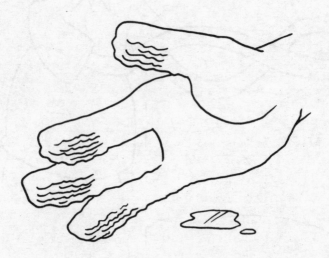

We think if we say it enough everyone will start
to use it,

even the queen.

OH, BOTHER . . .
FINKLES.

CHAPTER 3

Bella's **party** is two days away, so I want to be as **normal** as possible at school to make sure that she won't **un-invite** me.

This was going to be hard since today we were going on a school trip to the **ZOO** and Granddad was coming as a teacher's helper.

I knew it was going to be **trouble** when Granddad showed up at breakfast wearing fake **monkey ears**.

When we got on the **school bus**, Granddad took the empty seat next to Henry, and the only seat left for me was next to . . .

Bella.

I like Bella. I like her **a lot**. But I'm not sure if I'm ready to sit next to her on the bus.

We said hi . . .

HI. BELLA

. . . and that's it!

I didn't know what else to say to her. She didn't know what else to say to me. We just sat there **staring** at the back of the heads of the people in front of us!

Henry

Granddad/monkey

The sight of Granddad's **monkey ears** and Henry's **fuzzy orange hair** gave me an idea.

I took out my sketchbook and started **drawing** . . .

"What are you drawing?" Bella asked.

IT'S A MONKEYLION!

Bella reached down into her bag and pulled out a pair of **glasses**. She put them on and looked closely at my drawing.

HA! IT'S FUNNY.
YOU'RE A GOOD
DRAWER, WEIR.

I hadn't seen Bella wearing glasses before, and I must have been staring at them, because she noticed.

"The glasses are new," said Bella. "The eye doctor said I need to wear them when I'm looking at something closely."

"**Cool**," I said. "Can I try them on?"

SURE

She took them off and put them on **me**.

The glasses made **everything** look different.

They made Granddad's ears look

even bigger.

And Henry's head was **HUGE!**

You **do not** want to know what Toby Hogan looked like . . .

That was when Bella
asked me to **draw** her.

WEIR,
CAN YOU
DRAW ME?

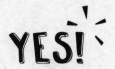

YES!

This was my chance to **impress** Bella with the one thing that I'm

<u>really</u> good at!

I picked up my sketchbook and pencil and started drawing Bella as well as I could.

When I finished, I showed her the picture of herself.

THAT'S . . . UMM, NICE, WEIR . . .

Bella said it was nice, but I don't think she meant it, because she had the same look on her face that Mum had when she found that **dead mouse** in the laundry basket . . .

THAT'S . . . UMM . . . NOT NICE.

Then I realized . . .

Oh no!

I **forgot** to take off the glasses, and they made me draw her **really ba_dly_**!

Oh man . . . What a way to start the day.

CHAPTER 4

When we got to the **zoo**, the first animals we saw were the **monkeys**.

I love monkeys, so me and Granddad went right up close to the fence.

I thought Granddad's monkey ears looked **silly**,
but the monkeys must have thought they looked
real, because the first thing that happened
was

a monkey

threw a banana

right at Granddad!

Granddad **ducked** out of the way.

Then I **ducked** out of the way.

And the **banana** hit Henry . . .

right in the face!

It was **sooo funny**, I started laughing.

I was **laughing**

so hard

I didn't see the **second banana** that was thrown.

Bella **ducked** it.

Blake **ducked** it.

Toby Hogan **ducked** it.

And it hit **me**
right on the side
of the head!

Now **everyone** was laughing at **me**!

Even Granddad!

HA HA HA HA HA HA

I guess it looked **pretty funny**!

As Henry and me stood there **flicking** the banana off ourselves, a whole bunch of **ducks** ran up to eat the bits off the ground.

They were funny, those ducks. Fat ones, skinny ones, and a big spotty one.

The **spotty** one had three little ducklings following it,

which was **very cute**.

Bella gave me a **hanky** to wipe myself. "Here you go, Weir," she said.

"Thanks," I said. And that's when I realized the hanky had **little frogs** on it.

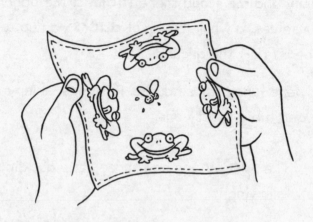

I looked up, and Bella was **smiling**.

Soon it was lunchtime, which was perfect, because I had heaps of ideas for **cool animal pictures**. First I tried a

giraffe and a **kangaroo**.

A Giraffaroo!

A **zebra** and an **elephant** . . .

A Zelephant!

A **panda** and a **gorilla** . . .

A Pandarilla!

But then I decided I wanted to try another drawing of Bella. I quickly drew her while she watched Henry

pretending he was a

sea lion.

I was pretty happy with my drawing and knew Bella would like it much more than the last one.

But as I went to hand it to her,

the **skinny duck** waddled over and

► **snatched it**

away from me! ⟫⟫⟫

213

Before I knew it, Bella had jumped up and was chasing after the duck with my drawing in its bill!

I ran after her.

I might have mentioned that I'm **not** a very fast runner . . .

And it turns out that duck was a
<u>ve</u>ry fast waddler! »»»

We chased that duck down past
the **gorilla** enclosure, »»»

through the **bat** cave, >>>>

along the **penguin** pool . . . >>>>

But then we lost the duck around

the **meerkat** bend.

Not only had we lost the duck,

but now **we were lost**, too!

We couldn't find Granddad, Miss Franklin, or anyone from school . . .

so we found **the next BEST thing** . . .

"Hey," said Bella, "what are you going to wear to **my party**?"

Huh? I thought to myself.

YOU KNOW IT'S A DRESS-UP PARTY, DON'T YOU?

"Oh yeah," I replied. "Sure . . . I'm going to go as . . ."

"So what was your drawing of, anyway?" asked Bella.

"Oh, nothing," I replied. "Just an—"

"**BELLA ALLEN!**" the zoo loudspeaker suddenly boomed.

BELLA ALLEN,
PLEASE RETURN TO
THE ZOO KIOSK
TO MEET YOUR TEACHER,
MISS FRANKLIN.

"AND WEIRDO!" the loudspeaker continued.

HAS ANYONE SEEN
A WEIRDO?
HE WAS LAST SEEN
WEARING A BLUE SHIRT,
GREY SHORTS, AND HIS
BIG SISTER'S SHOES.
COULD WEIRDO PLEASE RETURN
TO THE MONKEY
ENCLOSURE?

Everyone at the zoo laughed.

All the animals, too.

The **monkeys** . . .

223

The **penguins** . . .

Even the **duck** with the **glasses**!

I wanted to run away and hide, but before I could make a move, Granddad appeared.

I KNEW I'D FIND YOU NEAR THE FROGS!

The day at the zoo

wasn't a <u>complete</u> disaster.

On my way out, I found the *perfect* **birthday present** for Bella in the gift shop . . .

TWO
ROBOTS

At school the next day, Miss Franklin told us that we all needed to draw a picture of someone else in the class.

Here was my chance to draw Bella again!

But then Bella asked **Henry** if **he** would be her partner!

HENRY.
HENRY.
HENRY!!!

So I wound up with Clare instead . . .

I thought I'd done a

 pretty good job

of my drawing .

229

Henry's drawing of Bella was **even** <u>**worse**</u> than mine from the bus!

After school, Henry invited me over to his place to work on our **costumes** for Bella's party.

Henry was going as a **computer**. He put a box on his head, and I helped him attach a keyboard to his chest. When we finished, he looked like a human iPad.

He had lots of green cardboard for me to use to make a frog hat.

Perfect!

When we were finished, Henry showed me his **COLLECTION OF ROCKS** that he'd made to look like things . . .

Double-decker bus

Rock

Chicken

Half an elephant

. . . and then he introduced me to his sister.

"**WEIRDO?**" said Jane. "That's not very nice."

"Oh, no, that's his name," said Henry.

"Yeah, it's actually my name," I said.

WEIRD, ISN'T IT?

Then I met Henry's twin brothers. They looked **exactly** the same!

"I can see that," I said.

They even **talked** the same.

PEOPLE SAY
THEY CAN'T TELL
US APART.

PEOPLE SAY THEY
CAN'T TELL US
APART.

I couldn't tell them apart!

WE ARE DIFFERENT IN SOME WAYS, THOUGH.

WE ARE DIFFERENT IN SOME WAYS, THOUGH.

HE LIKES TO EAT GREEN M&M'S, AND
I LIKE TO EAT BLUE M&M'S.

YEAH. HE LIKES TO EAT BLUE M&M'S, AND I LIKE TO EAT GREEN M&M'S.

It was like looking at **two robots**.

Then Henry's mum and dad and their dog came out.

So this is what a **normal family** looks like!

"It's dinnertime, boys," said Mr O'Henry.
"Come join us at the table."

My mum's and dad's dinners **never**
look how they're supposed to.

How spaghetti is supposed to look.

How Mum's spaghetti looks.

How a Sunday dinner is supposed to look.

How Dad's Sunday dinner looks.

How noodles are supposed to look.

How Granddad's "noodles" look.

. . . but they **always** taste **delicious**!

But Mrs O'Henry's roast looked **just like** the picture in the book!

YUUUUUM!

This is going to be **SUPER yummy**, I thought to myself.

Shame it **tasted** like **cardboard**!

BIG CUCUMBER!

oder is Bella's **birthday party**!

Bella's present is
wrapped . . .

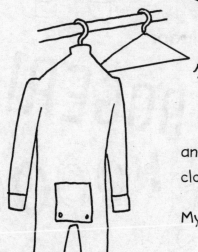

and my **green**
clothes are ready . . .

My **frog** hat is—

"**HEY**," I said, "where's my frog hat?"

Then I heard a

TERRIBLE

SPLASH!

coming from the **bathroom**.

Where my frog hat SHOULD have been!

ROGER!

NOOOOO

I ran to the bathroom, but it was **too late**.
My frog hat was already

sinking

in

bathwater...

I fished it out, and it

fell apart

in my hands.

I looked at Roger...

=CLEAN!=

OOOOO!

WEIR,
YOU CAN STILL
WEAR YOUR
GREEN
PYJAMAS.

"I can't just wear green," I complained. "I'll look like a **BIG** cucumber!"

Great, I get invited to Bella's party, and now I can't even go . . .

Then Sally stepped into the bathroom with an **"excellent idea."**

I HAVE AN EXCELLENT IDEA!

253

She pointed to the piles and piles of
toilet paper rolls in the corner.

Sally is supposed to be the **clever** one,
but this was the

worst idea ever!

"Sally, I'm **not** going as **toilet paper**!" I said.

Sally groaned. "No, we can wrap you with it, like a **mummy**!"

She picked up a roll and started **spinning** me around and around and around . . . and when I finally stopped whirling, I looked in the mirror and saw . . .

a really

COOL

mummy!

"Not bad," I said. "Thanks!"

So we're finally on our way to Bella's place, when we start

running out of gas.

But instead of stopping at the first gas station we see, Dad wants to wait until we come across a **cheaper** one!

Sometimes Dad can be **just as thrifty** as Mum!

Can you guess what happened next?

We ran out of petrol!

So Dad orders us all out, to help **push** >>> the car,
while Granddad runs off to get us a can of petrol.

First my **frog hat** gets destroyed, then our **car
runs out of petrol** on our way to the party . . .

What could be worse?

RAIN!

Rain could be worse!

Granddad came back with petrol, just as the rain stopped. But I no longer looked like a mummy . . .

I looked like a kid who'd been

FLUSHED down the toilet!

And my hands were covered in

FINKLES!

"What now?" I asked my genius sister.

DON'T ASK ME!

I climbed back into the car. I looked in the book behind me and saw the mega bag of **crisps** and the huge pack of **safety pins** that Roger had snuck into Mum's trolley.

Roger's shopping had just given **me**

\ \ I I I /
a BRILLIANT idea!
/ I \ \ \ \

I turned myself into a **vending machine**!

my →
vending
machine
costume

real vending machine

Everyone <u>**loved it**</u>, especially Bella's mum.
She'd forgotten to pick up all the **party snacks**,
so I'd arrived at just the right time . . .

MINE!
CRISPS!
OOH!
YUM!
MMM
CRISPS!
SALT AND VINEGAR!
YUM!
MY FAVOURITE!

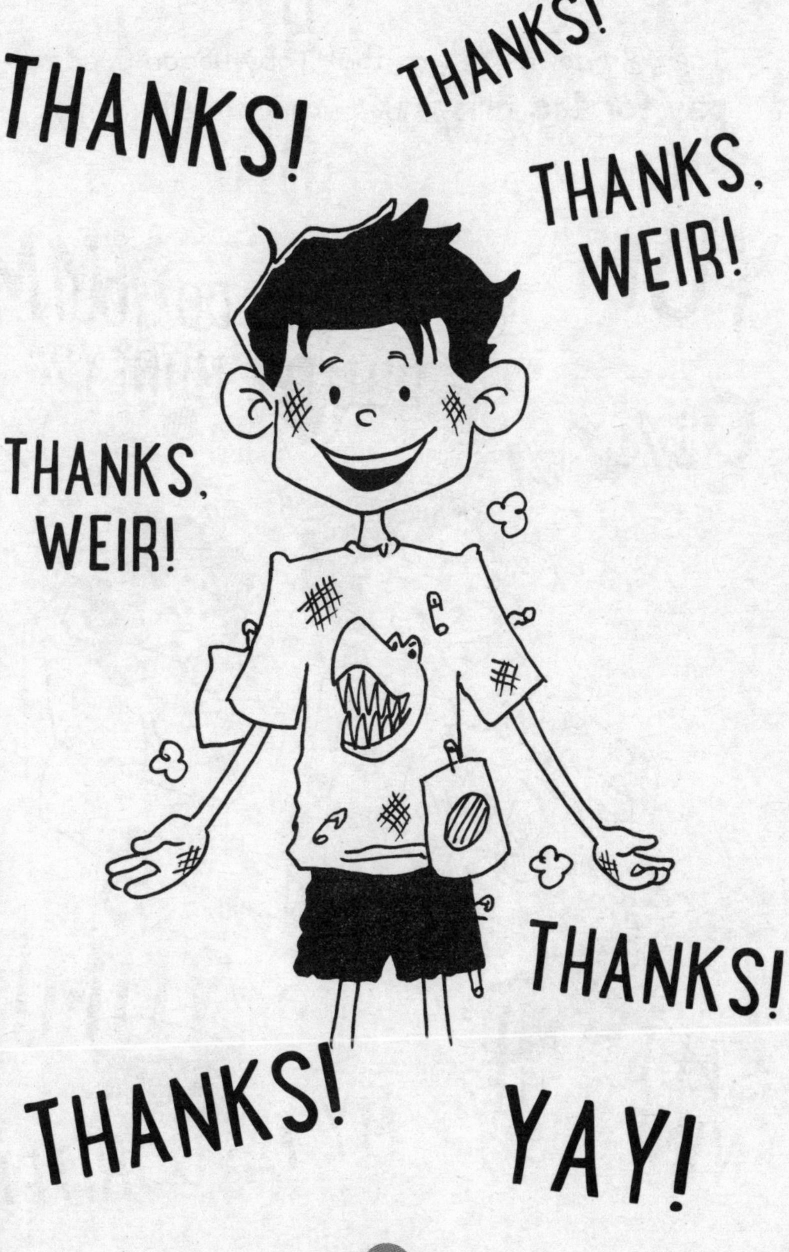
THANKS!
THANKS!
THANKS, WEIR!
THANKS, WEIR!
THANKS!
THANKS!
YAY!

The only downside was that Toby Hogan tried to **pay for the crisps** by putting a **coin** in my **ear**...

There was supposed to be a **magician** at the party, but he couldn't come because his **rabbit** had **eaten** his car keys.

But that didn't matter too much, because there was something at the party that turned out to be **much more fun** than a magician.

My crazy, <u>weird</u> family.

Granddad was up first to do some tricks. He pulled out his teeth . . .

I CAN MAKE MY TEETH
DISAPPEAR!

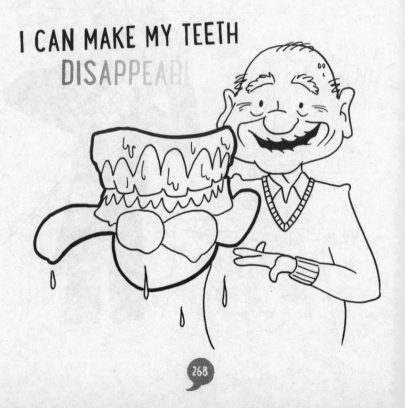

Then he made them _ _ _ _ _ _ !
↙ vanish

WOW!

Next, he said,

WATCH MY
MAGIC
ELBOW.

Then **Dad** was up.

I NEED A
SODA

UH-OH.

I started to **panic**. What was he going to do?

Dad burped his way through

HAPPY BIRTHDAYYY

273

Then some **music** came on the radio and
Dad started doing his

<u>horsey</u> dance.

Roger

Toby Hogan

Mary

Mullet

Sa

Soon **EVERYONE** was joining in.

Bella

Me

Granddad

Mum

Dad

Next, **Sally** started making some **cool balloon animals** for everyone.

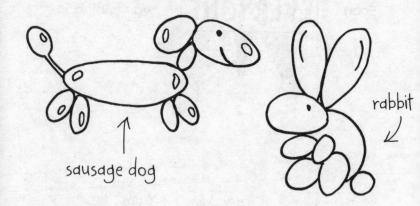

↑
sausage dog

rabbit
↙

Then I made the only **balloon animal** that I knew how to.

IT'S A SNAKE!

↙
snake

276

Then I came up with

another GREAT idea!

I tied **my snake** to **Sally's rabbit** and made
a **super-cool** animal.

snabbit

A SNABBIT!

THE
BEST

CHAPTER 8

It was turning out to be a **great party**! I did a **BIG drawing** and we had a game of

pin the tail on the
donkey-potamus

Roger helped Bella blow out her birthday candles, and Granddad **laughed** so loudly that his teeth

flew out

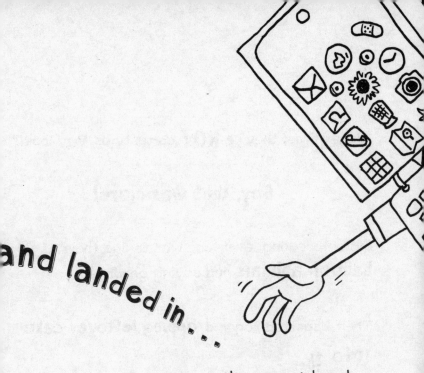

and landed in . . .

the sweet bowl.

Henry thought they were **candy teeth**
and was just about to **grab** them, when I
scooped them up. "HENRY!
                    HENRY!!
                        HENRY!!!" I said.

"Huh?"

"Believe me, they're **NOT** as tasty as they look!"

Boy, that was close!

But before long, everyone was taking their **balloon animals** and saying goodbye.

Then I spotted Roger **dropping leftover cake into the fruit juice.**

CLEAN!

I was trying to **scoop** the cake out, when Bella came up to us.

"He is **sooooo** cute," said Bella.

Cute? Roger?

I handed him to Mum.

"I'm really glad you came to my party, Weir," Bella added. "You know, your drawing of Clare yesterday was **really nice**."

"Thanks," I said.

"You drew me, on the bus, but I guess I'm not as nice-looking as her . . ."

HUH?
OH NO, YOU ARE!
I JUST . . .
IT WAS . . .

THE PROBLEM WAS YOUR GLASSES . . .

OH, YOU DON'T LIKE MY GLASSES?

NO, NO, I WAS WEARING YOUR GLASSES

... THAT'S WHY I DREW YOU FUNNY. I COULDN'T SEE PROPERLY!

"Oh!" said Bella.

"Hey, I almost forgot to give you this," I said, remembering the present in my pocket that I'd found for her at the zoo.

First, Bella opened the **card** I'd made her.

Bella blushed and gave me a **great big smile**.

I'm a bit short and I can't run very fast, but I'm **lucky** I can draw.

She opened the present next.

WOW, I LOVE IT!

"Thanks, Weir," she said. "**You're the best**. And thanks for **saving** my party. It looked like it was going to be a disaster . . .

... UNTIL YOU AND YOUR FAMILY SHOWED UP.

Phew. I'd made it through my **first birthday party** with my <u>new</u> friends.

And the **seventh-best-looking girl** in school just called me

THE BEST.

Me!

<u>Weir Do!</u>

MORE
TO COME!

For my three **boys**

who helped me with
this book . . .

FROM ANH

★ Henry's **funny-looking**
mum and dad, based on
drawings by **Xavier Do**

★ Henry's **strange** twin brothers,
based on drawings by **Luc Do**

★ **Blockhead** the parrot's crazy
habits, suggested by **Leon Do**